Paper Boats

Poems by Hilary Tham

An Original by Three Continents Press

©1987 Hilary Tham

A Three Continents Book

Published in the United States of America by
Lynne Rienner Publishers, Inc.
1800 30th Street, Boulder, Colorado 80301

ISBN: 0-89410-541-8 (cloth)
0-89410-542-6 (paper)
LC No.: 86-50769

Cover art © 1987 by Max K. Winkler

Acknowledgments

Grateful acknowledgment is given to the following publications where poems in this collection first appeared or are to appear, occasionally in other versions:

Ariel, "Three Revolts of Miss Maybury"; **Phoebe**, "Mrs. Wei and the Thief"; **Poet Lore**, "Letter from Malaysia"; **Monthly Bulletin of Vietnam Veterans of America, Ch. 43**, "Cambodian Refugees"; **Waterways**, "Superstition", "Miss Maybury Takes a Nap", "Birthright", "Ch'ng Ming II", "Grandfather Au", "Grandfather on an October Day", "Mrs. Wei Refuses to Bury Her Grandmother", "Soldiers' Cemetery, Kuala Lumpur"; **Apogee—Microcosm**, "Spacey Spiders", "Science Fiction Fantasia"; **E.D. Studies**, "Portrait of Miss Emily Dickinson"; **World's Word**, "Father"; **Windfall**, "Seeds".

"Superstition" was reprinted in **ESRA**, Israel, and in **Wineberry Press—Poems on Postcards**.

"Seeds" and "Mrs. Wei and the Thief" were reprinted in the anthology **Snow Summits in the Sun**, Cerulean Press, California; and "The Boy", "Mrs. Wei on the Bus", "Mrs. Wei and the Beggar", "Night of the Barbarian", "Working Women", "Golden Lilies", and "Family Fight" first appeared in the same anthology.

"Grass" appeared in the anthology **The Second Tongue: An Anthology of Poetry from Malaysia and Singapore** © Heinemann Educational Books (Asia), 1976.

"The Pawnbroker's" and "crows in the cemetery" appeared in the chapbook **No Gods Today** © Hilary Tham, 1969.

My thanks to Random House, Inc. for permission to reprint the lines from "Canzone" from **W.H. Auden: Collected Poems**, edited by Edward Mendelson, © Random House, Inc.

Thanks also to Elisavietta Ritchie, the Macomb Street Gang poets, Gallant Hall poets, Professor Isaac Goldberg, Nancy Ivins and Ann Wintermute for their special help. My gratitude to the Goldbergs: Joe, Ilana, Shoshana and Rebecca for putting up with me while I write.

for my parents, Au Lin Tei and Tham Sun Hong
and my sisters, my brothers
for my people and my culture

". . . in whose mirror I begin to know
the chaos of the heart . . ."

W.H. Auden—**Canzone**

Table of Contents

I. Rice Field/1

II. Ghost Trees/35

III. Mrs. Wei's Garden/55

IV. Private Landscape/73

V. Caves/81

I

RICE FIELD

The Arranged Marriage

Those rare nights my father
did not leave the house to find
women who decanted soft laughter
to feast him, he paced, agitated
as a tailless lizard on the ceiling.
My mother sat, quietly sewing
clothes for the children.

Sometimes he told us stories:
the beautiful ghost who had no feet,
the absent-minded English Tuan
who offered him a tow, then tried
to outrace him and rollercoastered him
cursing and honking past havens
of filling stations.

Mother no longer laughed at his stories.
She saw him through a fret of unpaid
landlords, gonorrhea afflictions,
five needy children, the pain
of a sixth child dying.
They wept when Sister died. Separately.

Night after night, she sat and sewed
patchwork blankets, stitched and knotted
nets of binding for her children.
My father did not notice until
his nights grew old. When he turned
to her, she had no cloth left,
only needles in her mending basket.

Superstition

The Chinese believe our dead return
as white butterflies on happy occasions,
to shed a blessing on the birth of sons,
to drink the moist scents of bridal teas.

White butterflies never appear at funerals
or at the pitch of familial battles
when Father smashed chairs and china
and Mother wielded words with equal violence.

Sister died young. I grew and left home.
The first time I returned, with my children,
Father was proud, Mother jubilant.
A white butterfly flew into the house.

Village Afternoons

Under the tamarind tree
by the family woodpile,
we sweated and split
mangrove logs for cook-fires.
Some days Mother doused our heads
with kerosene, picked lice
from our hair.

Once a month the travelling barber
came, hung his bronze mirror
on the tamarind tree. We played
stone - water - bird to see
who went under his shears next,
then watched the hair fall,
black talcum on brown dirt.

One rainy day a mad woman came.
She stood under the tree rolling
her eyes, swinging a rope. We wondered
if she would hang herself. Mother said
she was a new neighbor searching
for her dog.

Under the tamarind tree one noon,
in our woodpile, Old Mr. Tao found
a nest of pink baby mice.
He shouted with delight and ran
for his three-stars-brandy.
Then he ate them alive.

Paper Boats

Monsoon season. The rain,
copious and hot, churned dirt
into treacle streams that joined and grew
a mud-brown river at our doorsill.
My sisters and I folded paper into sampans
to launch upon its ripples. Ducks were out,
one duck especially loud as she snaked
her head from side to side, butted
her yellow babies into the water.

Our parents sat indoors, built walls
of mahjong tiles. Their talk
eddied above our heads—Widow Ho's lover,
the price of rice, Singapore chickens,
Chuang-tzu's wife fanning his grave,
the ghost in Wu Mansion glided
over our understanding as our boats over
the water. We were aware
only of their voices, not knowing
ripples on the water will shape
patterns deep below.

Darkness and distance stole our boats.
We curled into bed cocooned in blankets,
mosquito netting, walls, the rain quilting
on our tin roof.

I thought of Grandfather, the rain
soaking his grave. His parents could not
know their son would not return to China,
that his bones would lie in Klang's hills, washed

grain by grain into another sea.
They stood on Canton's docks, forever
watched one boat going, growing
small like a toy,
beyond their watching, beyond
stretch of their eyes, center
of ripples they would never see.

Family Fight

When I was nine, Father
and Mother walked out on us,
each swearing never to return.
The neighbors flapped about,
laying words in their path.
In their anger, we were not their children
but weapons to use against the other.
All five of us ran after them
casting their names like nets
and stopped by the gate, unable
to choose the parent to pursue.

Once in a happier time
when they were pleasant together,
we visited a ruined temple.
Its once-white walls were charred,
their blood-red bricks exposed,
the courtyard littered with roof tiles,
pieces of broken gods.

Our parents returned the next day.
They continued, unhappy with each other
while I gathered fractured gods
in dreams of abandoned temples.

Dowry

For my wedding my mother gave me
two jade rings, a skirt of crimson silk,
two red woolen blankets trimmed
with green thread for luck
and fertility, six pairs of ivory
chopsticks and a large steel wok.

"To cook with all your days.
To protect when evil spirits
sniff your footprints.
Blacked by fire, this wok will turn
ghosts from your house.
Set it bottom side up in your door
should you feel haunted."

So I came to America carrying a wok.
My veins carried thin blue milk
from my mother's carefully hidden breasts.
She had nursed me herself, she said.
She also ascribed my height
to cow's milk imported from England.
I could not decide which history
to believe. Sometimes at five in the morning
I believed both.

My Grandmother's Curse

My grandmother had huge teeth
gleaming ivory on pink.
                     I'd watch them
bite deep into a hunk
of new baked bread
                  and stay there
abandoning her mouth
an O of disappointed
                    anticipation.
"Fuck it" she would mumble.

My grandmother had small hands
stained with tobacco juice.
                     I'd watch them
roll a pinch in cheap cigarette paper
stick the stubby result
in her mouth and flare
                  a sulphurous match.
Two puffs before her smoke died
in the spittle-soaked middle.
"Fuck it" she grumbled.

The Fang War

Mother warned us. The gang
on our street, the Eighteen Saints,
prepared for war. They honed
their parangs, brought staffs
and hammers, put new edges
on their knives. We peered
behind shutters as they passed
with axes, choppers, pike
handles of ironwood.

We were told to come home
straight from school, to stay
indoors. The Eighteen
Saints prepared for war.

Each afternoon we heard
sounds of metal clashing
on wood, "Heiiya!" explosions
from Tae Kwan-do manoeuvres,
grunts as flesh met pain.
The Eighteen Saints prepared for war.

One of the Saints, Lovesick
Fang, had secretly courted
a cousin of the Kapir Road Tong.
They had beaten him
black and green, dumped him
at the Chief Saint's door
in a dark hour of morning.
So the Eighteen prepared
for war.

The challenge was sent,
the date fixed. Word came
to stay indoors. We woke
to sounds we had heard all week—
thuds, grunts, "Heiiya" screams.
Then police whistles shrilled,
feet pounded past into the jungle
behind our house. Policemen came,
asked questions. No one knew about
gangs in our neighborhood.

Next morning we heard
the Saints had won. The police looked
in vain for wounded warriors;
many sons from both streets
were "out-of-town."

The Eighteen Saints had taught
the Tong "a lesson in manners
and territorial law." Lovesick
was ordered to stay within
Saints' territory for safety.
We played on our street again.

Fang hung around, carved hearts
on our tamarind tree. We chanted
"Fang's in love! Lovesick Fang!"
but he would not chase us.

He had spun tops with Eldest
Brother when they were boys.
Together they cadged ice
from "Rich Mrs. Peng,"
she had a refrigerator.

Together they explored
the forbidden jungle
behind our house, came home
covered with leeches.
Leeches black and shiny
that Mother burned off
with Grandmother's cigars
before she sent Fang home
and brought out the stick
to chastise Eldest Brother.

Fang's mother cried when he
became a Saint. Eldest Brother
went away to college.
He rarely came home, and was not
interested or pretended
disinterest when we chattered
our news. He did not visit
during the Fang War.

Once a month, a Saint came
to collect "protection money."
Mother served him tea and rice-cake,
talked about the weather.
Fang never came to collect.
Mother would have nagged
him to leave the Gang.

His girl came a few times.
The Saints frowned, but they
left her alone. Fang still carved
hearts on our tree, still ignored us.
Then he was not around anymore.

The Saints found him sliced up,
decapitated in the schoolyard,
neutral ground. He had made
a secret trip to the Kapir Road
Cinema for a Clint Eastwood movie.
The enemy had spotted him,
caught him on their ground.

Tha Saints raged and cursed,
but they did not bring out weapons.
Gang law was law: Fang had trespassed,
they could not prepare for war. Instead,
they buried him with full honors,
and played, on flutes and gong,
"Coffin for a Gunfighter."

Golden Lilies

Grandmother could swear the air purple
and black. My parents became
meeker than white mice when she
stamped her foot in anger.
She had tiny feet and wore size four
in children's shoes.

She hated hospitals. Their smells
snarled and trapped her again
in the childhood terror when
the footbinder smashed a mallet
on her toes, crushed her feet,
squeezed them into taut red silk strips
that were tightened each week.
The smell of decay
meshed with the pain forever
and hospital smells triggered
agony in her mind's unbound flesh.

The Doll

Mother said:
"I cannot afford to buy one
but I will make you a doll."

2 popsicle sticks
crossed and tied with string.
2 eyes with brows pencilled in.
A quick stroke of another pen
made a scarlet smiling mouth. Then
a dab of glue and cotton wool.
2 scraps of cloth from the sewing
basket, with lace tacked on.

And Doll was fully formed, with
a change of clothes to hand.

Doll lived under my pillow for years.
She did not meet the porcelain
doll, the plastic dolls on our street.
They had real hair, hands with fingers
and toes on their feet.

Mr. Lee Tak

His mother sold him at age three
to provision his father's funeral.
His new family was rich but acted poor,
praised habits of thrift he did not learn.
Craving honey, he fell from trees,
armies of bees swarming in retribution.

He adored Catholic churches; secretly
pinched his personal tithe
from the collection plate
to enlarge his allowance.
The deacon looked the other way
for the child with the charming eyes.

Magnanimity suited him. He loved
the power to create warmth with lavish
tips, extravagance. He lived, loved well,
spent exceedingly, borrowed easily,
died cheerful, was buried cheaply.
His wife refused to sell a child for his funeral.

Father

1

It was better than carnival day to see
you in the opera, slender in
a gown of sequined silk, diamond
pins in your elaborate wig, your hands
arcing in grace-lineated gestures
as your voice stroked and stretched,
fish glistening upstream
against the roaring of cymbals.

Older, your waist thickened,
you played the hero, strode high
over invisible doorsills, rode unseen horses,
made invisible cities fall
with serpentine ripplings of flags while drums
pounded through my ears and my blood.
Later you played the saxophone in the band.
I knew you could do anything.

2

My first memory is you, playing
with me and Sister who died.
You sloped a plywood board,
conjured Monte Carlo's Grand Prix
for our little lead cars.
You were commentator and sound effects
and we were squeals and admiration.

3

Those were rain days in our growing season,
and rare. You sowed and followed
the freedom of butterflies, abandoned us
for flights with beautiful women.
Returning for the harvest, you are surprised
there are blackbirds in your ricefield.

Port Swettenham, Malaya

Grandfather Au came from Canton
in a boatload of men hungry for jobs
and money to send home. He worked
the wooden hulls of ships
anchored by the jungle's edge.

The port was a dozen shacks
under flame trees, walkways skirting
the green water. Walkways in mangrove
trees whose roots they hacked
each Sunday to clear the water
for tramp ships, cargo boats
carrying India tea, silk from China.

He told me over cups of steamy
black tea how he'd strip down,
tie a rope and his tools
round his waist and plunge off a ship,
half his time rising for air,
plummeting down again.

At dinner he shovelled rice into his mouth
from his blue enamel bowl, chopsticks
a steady flick-flack.
Afterwards I'd hear how
under water, he hammered
new wood over rotted spots,
make-shift until home port.

The flame trees are gone now.
The port is grey concrete
with corrugated zinc warehouses, asphalt roads.
Grandfather did not live to see it.

In the eight years our lives overlapped,
he crafted cabinets, tables, chairs
and never swam in the sea.

Grandfather Au

His funeral was a splendid ceremony
with gongs and drums shaking the ground.
The coffin was handcarved mahogany;
our house thrummed, neighbors came around
to swirl up trays of food to feast and pay
the crowds who came to entertain the night
and parade with him the following day.
He slept through the noise and the light.

On Sunday I looked for him to bring
the packaged surprise he like to dangle
wrapped in newspaper, tied with string,
tantalizing knots for me to untangle.
He never came. I mourned waiting by the gate
knowing his funeral final and I was late.

Grand-Uncle Soong's Wisdom

Uncle Soong hid all the brooms
at New Year in case "some fool
should sweep away the year's luck."

The rest of the year, he waved
his broom at cats that came
near the house, shouting:
"If a stray dog comes, that's luck!
The cat that seeks its own home
hides demons under its tail.
Chase it away!"

Uncle Soong slept in the hall.
In his bedroom, his special coffin
made of ironwood to cheat the termites
stood on trestles that warned us
children off with bristling splinters.
It was a beautiful coffin, shaped
like a boat, carved sides elaborate
with black and silver markings.

Uncle Soong polished that coffin
every day and slept in the hall
fifteen years. The house felt
emptied when the coffin went.

Su Mei

Su Mei going
to the bathroom
every ten minutes
knew she was dying,
slowly, quietly
flowing away while
the family was busy, unaware.

"What's the matter with
the girl?" Grandmother asked.
"Have you got diarrhea?"

"I'm hurt inside,"
Su Mei whispered, "I'm bleeding
to death." Grandmother
laughed and laughed.
"It's nothing special."

Su Mei did not die
though she wished she had.
Grandmother told this
as her best funny story
for years.

Lee Lee

Her mother fretted. Lee Lee at fifteen
was still a child. Her doctor prescribed
iodine pills.

Lee Lee tagged behind the girls
in the school playground, kept out
on the edge of friendships, unable
to participate in the giggles, the whispers,
jokes about Moses and the Red Sea,
elephant eggs. The girls smiled
at her, would not explain.

One afternoon, blood blossomed
for her. Her mother rejoiced:
her grave would be visited, grandsons
danced in her vision.

Lee Lee bent to the sink, its whiteness
made terrible the red blood.
She turned on the faucet, watched
the crimson pale with running water,
watched it spill into darkness
below the drain. In that darkness
she saw falling the petals
of blown bougainvilleas, felt
unfurling in her body
tendrils of decay.

Becoming a Woman

When I was twelve, my mother initiated me
into the mysteries of becoming a woman
with a pound of rice-paper, the unadvertised
kind made from stalks and leaves, the stubble
after the harvest.

She taught me the art of crumpling,
stretching, folding the sheafs into
a likeness of Modess-factory-rejects.

          "You will bleed
at a special time of the moon,"
she told me. "Use these
to preserve modesty and the secret
of your femaleness."

Her mother's way she passed to me
with the few words she had received
at her initiation.

Each full moon I cursed the tides
within my body. I abandoned
tradition's rice-paper.

I have forgiven the moon since
our children came, spores of sunrise
in their newborn hands.

Letter from Malaysia

I have arranged a marriage, my mother wrote,
for your sister and the third son
of the Tong family. He is single
and he died ten years ago. Your sister
liked him at the Viewing Ceremony,
the medium said, and promises to behave
once she is wed. It has been a terrible time
since your brother's wedding. Sickness
in the house, his bride screaming each night
in her sleep, their dreams troubled by fingers
squeezing their throats.

In secret I went to the Temple,
begged Kuan Yin's help. The medium said
it was your sister, eighteen years quiet
in her grave, roused by her brother's marriage,
desires her own.

You know your brother. He laughs at me
and my faith. I tell him nothing.
I tell you because she would like you
to know and rejoice at her happiness.
You were so close in her life.

One other thing: your brother's wife
has stopped screaming in her sleep since
the marriage was announced to the ancestors.

Thank the Goddess everyone is healthy now.

Real Estate

For years my grandparents grudged
each dollar they spent on rent,
pickled vegetables and rice in Malaya, sent
his pay to the land agent in China.
At dark, they doused the kerosene lamp
and went to bed. There they strolled
through Kwangtung Province, lords of land.
Clad in clean cotton gowns, they paced
every foot of land they would own,
their rough sun-darkened hands growing
    white and soft with idleness.
And the rice grew tall before their eyes.

After the Great Revolution, when landlords in China
became bastard dogs stoned out of every village,
they joined the burial society of Klang.
Grandmother began to buy meat,
she learnt to play mahjong.
Grandfather bought a wall-scroll—
    a painted landscape: Yangtze mountains
        unattainable peaks above clouds, gorges
            hidden behind mists—
to look at in the long nights.

Ch'ng Ming I
(Festival of the Dead)

Great-grandmother's grave in the oldest part
of the cemetery is an enormous mound
five feet high, yet not the highest here.
A great place to play hide-go-seek
while parents picnic with the old lady.

Mother's parents have modest graves
only two feet high like all the mounds
in their part of the cemetery.
We make rock gardens on our visit.

Paternal Grandmother died recently.
Her grave is almost flat, though the tombstone
is tall in the old style. There are graves
here with small modern headstones. We have

eaten so much at the other graves we
can only sip tea to keep Grandmother
company while she shares our picnic.
We never visit Sister's grave.

Mother says she does not remember
where it is. There are no markers
in the tall grass of
the children's field.

Grandfather on an October Day

Throughout dinner
you spoke in past tenses.
You did not eat much, though we
heaped your bowl. Mainly you
reminisced, recalled the hot
afternoon you took me fishing:
how we caught fifteen sleepy catfish
in a monsoon drain, other catches
with friends now dead. You did not
seem sad, though you said
you were tired tonight
and would retire early.
You folded your napkin
with deliberation. The veins
on the backs of your hands
stood like bark on the backyard raintree.
Were your hands paler or the agespots
darker or just a trick of the light?
Why did I think of silences,
the stillness of cars in procession,
headlights beating a path through the rain
to a newly dug hole, when you said
your usual "Goodnight, all"?

Looking up at you as you rose
from the table, your rice half
eaten, the chocolate cake yet uncut,
I thought I saw threads breaking,
floating around your familiar head.
It must have been stray hairs
catching the light at odd angles.

The children ran into your room,
cajoling you into sing-song games.
When I finally knocked
at your door and sent them to bed,
you stood in their tumbling wake
to say good night again. I too was tired,
my eyes ached. That must have been
why I fancied I saw
wrinkles fade from your face
and earth-colored vines behind your head.

Conversations With Mother

I.

You told me I was born at home.
Home was a house with dirt
floors and a coffin in the back room:
Grand-uncle's life insurance.
Grandmother was displeased.

"A girl! a good-for-nothing
girl!"
        But you were glad.

You told me many times: each time
Father took a new mistress,
when Sister died, when I became
a Catholic, when I became a Jew,
when I had daughters and felt
a Chinese guilt;
each time you felt I needed
to know I had a place
in your house.

II.

The words I use
contain your tones, your thinking.

Words I do not remember hearing
haunt my ears.

I read your letters eagerly now.
Distance makes scarcity, makes precious

your words that were once walls
I ran past to get to the door.

III.

Home is an unfamiliar house.
I have lived away so long
I cannot find the drawer
where the chopsticks lie
ivory smooth upon each other.
I hand you a fork and you
accept it awkwardly.

In your mind you revise your will,
seeing the last step of that first
step you took when you handed me,
self-consciously seven, to strangers
in white robes and wimples. You
accept at last I cannot
inherit your house.

Mother, I've got all the houses
you've lived in packed
into my suitcase.

Hands

My mother had hands that could
cocoon my head, leaving peepholes
between fingers for my eyes.
I saw them as two continents
with networks of pink rivers
in white mountains.

The rivers, mountains shrank
like ground falling
from a rising hawk
as I climbed the years.
I saw at last her hands
small as sparrows darting about
my shoulders, straw words
and clay hopes clutched in the beaks
arrowed on my back.

II

GHOST TREES

Advice to Travellers

If you go
into wayside woods,
make noise,
crush bracken,
whistle a noisy tune.
Do not step
on the nose
of an earth godling
asleep in the ground.
Give the tree spirit a chance
to move before
you piss on his foot.

If you offend
a petty god with
a human indignity, he could
pluck a hair
from his scalp and stick it
in your rib
to canker and spread
till you are dead,
or wish you were.

The Chinese Mind

is happily
illogical and
compart-
mentalized.
One part believes
in the Eighteen
Hells, one for
each specific sin.

Gluttony's Hell
has small black imps
who vivisect
the victim over
and over and
make blood-sausages
with his intestines.

The Hell for Liars
has big red devils.
They chop up
the sinner's tongue
inch by inch as it
regenerates.

The Buddhist
section of the mind
drums out messages
of reincarnation.
"Righteous living
earns rebirth as a man."
Less will make you

a woman. Bad becomes
a dog, a cow, a cat . . .
down through snakes,
worms to the lowly insect.
Eighty lifetimes to climb
up to humanity again.
"Try for Nirvana now!"

This use of moral
carrot and stick
seems to work.
We have an earned
reputation
for hard work,
uprightness
and, it follows,
inscrutability
since our motives
are seldom apparent,
even to ourselves.

Fox Maiden

"... a young woman believed to be possessed by a 'fox spirit' responsible for reducing the sexual ability of young men was battered to death in the southern province of Guangdong."

The Washington Times, *February 4, 1986*

Speculation:

I see the witch-hunter, mouth
piece of the gods, sparse
hair twisted back,
breasts shrunken to raisins.
    She unhooks an arthritic finger,
points the rage that seeks
vulpine features, reddish hair.

Legend:

In abandoned temples, she smiles
over her shoulder, between rain-
eaten doors.
    He follows,
fumbles with the patchwork triangle
that hides her breasts.
        And the moonlight
cold as jade, binds him as he presses
her yielding flesh into courtyard stone;
weaves knots in his heart.
He stumbles forever through sunlight, lost
in moon mist, white breasts.

Ch'ng Ming II

In Spring
when flowers come out of the ground
to touch sunlight, the dead
hold "open house".

For three days, the living are welcome
to walk among the cemetery mounds,
smiling, to talk and wonder about
the lives compressed

in the small space on headstones.
A time to visit ancestors
and tidy their graves.

This insures their continued goodwill
and influence on the family's behalf.
All bring, as is only courteous,
gifts of food and silver and incense.

The Good Deed

Buddhist New Year.
Hunters have trapped birds and fish
and brought them in cartloads
from the hills.

We buy sparrows and pigeons,
we loose them from bamboo cages;
their wings rise with our prayers
for rebirth.

Some make it back to the hills,
escape the hunger of local hawks.
Our river is speckled with red
eyes of floating fish.

Fire Dance

On the fifteenth day of the ninth moon
the Chinese God of Oceans comes ashore.
In his newly painted statue, he rides
his red and black sedan-chair through the town.

His people greet him waving yellow kerchiefs.
They perfume the air with incense and faith.
They spread a feast of chickens brooding
on nests of saffron rice, eggs dyed pink.

Those who brave the fire-dance have abstained
from meat and other pleasures nine weeks.
They cross forty yards of burning coal barefoot;
unscorched feet the god's sign of pleasure.

Some ascribe this to salt in the sea-water
flung over the blaze before the ceremony.
But I have seen a few falter and break away,
seen their burns, their blistered soles.

These the monks bandage while the rest, jubilant,
dance the departing god down to the sea.
They will have nets filled with fish this year.
The god was pleased: so many with unmarked feet.

The Kitchen God

The Kitchen God is a gullible chap.
He'd swallow anything, especially sugar
in New Year cakes of sticky rice.
We give him these at the year's end.

Then he'll climb his sugarcane ladder,
make his annual report to Heaven.
He will tell kind and gentle lies
for his household's benefit.

A simpleton in his own life, he
starved to death, tricked of silver
his ex-wife sent in ricecakes.
He traded them for a bowl of noodles.

This fate pleased Heaven, somehow,
gave him a place near food, forever.

The Sky God

Keeps the universe in order,
each star in its space,
each sun burning, sets
the movement of moons and tides.
Sits above the echelon
of bribable gods who manage
Chinese affairs.

The Sky God
frowns on bribes.
Has no interest
in pagodas nineteen stories high
moated by pools where
century-old turtles chew
spinach stalks.

The Sky God
has no images, no statues,
just the Name in gold script
on red paper above the door.
Accepts offerings of incense,
candles, cups of tea sugared
by respect.

Legend of Mangku Maid

Mangku Maid so blind
crying "Husband before,
husband behind."
For the pun of a foolish tongue,
the Goddess was unkind.

Chin Shih Emperor decreed a Wall
fifteen hundred miles long
of grey stone
and white human bone
to safeguard his empire.

The Wall would not rise.
His seer called for ten thousand lives
as sacrifice. The people cried:
"Wan means ten thousand. A man
named Wan will save our lives."

They were newly wed:
Mangku Maid and Wan Shih-liang, when
the Emperor's soldiers came
and took her man
for the Wall.

First she wept and wrung her hands.
Then she rose and followed.
The way was rough and winter cold
but she would give Wan's spirit peace,
burial in a hometown grave.

She found his bones, she found them all.
She filled one basket, she filled two.
She hung them on a pole
over her right shoulder.
Her courage touched Goddess Kuan Yin.

Homeward bound, a basket before
and behind her, Mangku met
the Goddess disguised as busybody,
shrill crone intruding
on her sorrow.

What did she carry?
Would she re-marry?
Mangku answered impatiently,
not knowing a goddess came
to restore Wan's life.

Mangku Maid so blind
crying "Husband before,
husband behind."
For the pun of a foolish tongue
the Goddess was unkind.

Her words enraged Kuan Yin.
Shining tall, She shed her rags, told
the astonished cowering girl
the gift She now disdained to bestow.
Mangku had guilt added to sorrow.

Mangku Maid so blind
crying "Fu chien,
fu how."
For the pun of an impatient tongue,
the Goddess was unkind.

Birthright

Be sure to fold
the silver paper with matching points.
We cannot give the Yellow Emperor
crushed ingots.
The paper mansion must be put on the pyre
immediately after the body, a shelter
is most important, even after death.
Then the servants, the car.
Made of the best bamboo and black silk,
it looks like his favorite Mercedes.
Next, burn the chests of gold
and silver ingots. Then the Bank of Hell money.
Perhaps you should order more. Your father
was used to wealth. You must not stint
his endowment over there.

It is not a matter of belief.
This is your duty, your birthright.
Go through the motions. If you do not
buy water to wash his face,
close the skin over his eyes
and seal his lips with a silver coin,
his spirit cannot cross the Yellow Springs.
It will walk, tattered and torn,
stepping on the hem of your shadow
till shadow fires burn
every night behind your dreams.

Bribing the Gods

If you must offer a bribe
to a god to change the stars
in your zodiac, be careful
to pay your debt.
Remember to build the lotus pond
you promised Kuan Yin's temple,
even to stock it with carp
and the best flowering lotus.
The gods expect fair wages
for work done. A lotus pond
seemed fair price for the goddess's
intercession with the Yellow Emperor.
His dogs were sniffing
at your son's hospital bed.

Do not forget
that wayside god you promised to adopt
in exchange for a promotion.
Bring its statue home with ceremony
and drums or it will send a huge bill
to bankrupt your future.

If you must offer a bribe
to a god to change the stars
in your zodiac, be careful.

Snake Temple

There is a temple in Penang
where small grass snakes and
pythons hold court on tall stone
altars. They keep their eyes shut
but open their mouths to smell
the incense and worship of visitors
with their tongues.

Kuan Ti, god of war, sat here before.
With peace, the temple's power
and prosperity declined.
 A snake came,
slept on the altar and was declared
a new god-in-residence. All
snakes in the vicinity were
captured and worshipped.
Those with godhead stayed.

The nuns who ply their gods
with incense to make them sleep
and stay, look sleek and well-fed.
They raise chickens and crickets,
meat for the gods. They themselves
are vegetarians, eat only soybean
dishes they call mock abalone,
mock roast pig, mock duck.
As gods, snakes seem adequate.
Prayers are answered, often enough;
the temple's coffers are filled.

Laughing Buddha

I.

Most displaced of all the gods, he roams
the world, his smile still wide,
his belly round as a melon.

His statues are no longer bought
for family altars sweet with belief.
No temples bear his name.

His images, small and portable,
are sold to strangers. They take him
out on Bingo nights.

II.

His life-size statues used to dine
on whole roast suckling pigs, their
teeth clenched on red apples
and green chives. His faithful
filled his air with incense
and prayers, vying for his smile.

Now foreigners give his miniatures
crumbs of faith in Bingo halls
shrouded in cigarette smoke. His stomachs
shine from their rubbing
for that one lucky number. His companions
among chips and penny markers
are African skulls, wooden elephants,
paws slashed from lucky monkeys.

The Pawnbroker's

I passed his dingy shop
one rainy afternoon at Year's end.

I saw a lot of things, old
and new, mostly old

guitars, T.V.s, wedding rings
and watches under locked glass,

expressionless, passive, mute, but
not as mute as the Buddha

beside a pile of gaudy toys.
Someone had pawned his god.

The Fortune-Teller

Madame Chan keeps banker's hours,
has branch offices. Her clients, mainly women,
line up for number tags, talk about
her cures.
          The first is a girl
torturing daisies in mental meadows
(he loves me, he loves me not).
The line listens avidly for the answer.
"Lay your head peaceful
on your pillow, shake scorpions
from your hair, he is true to you."

A mother fears for her daughter's marriage.
In trance, the medium dispatches
her spirit to investigate, reports
the couple's home a battlefield,
petty gods jostling for position.
"Install a House God to govern them,
felicity will return."

Some ask for health, success and sons.
Madame Chan listens, dispenses hope
as the god pleases, counsels
lower expectations to others.

The god's image on the altar is huge,
his face fearsome, dark from constant incense.
But his eyes are benign as they look down
on his chosen, a short plump woman
made for loving and motherhood. Her hands
caress only yellow fu papers now,
writing his prescriptions which should be
burnt and taken with water before meals.

The Chinese Mind II

The Chinese Mind is curious
and ample, has a happy
anarchy of residents who make
room for any gods passing through.

Sweet Jesus is guested near
the Buddha and the Kitchen God.
The Door Gods sort memos: requests
from Ancestors who want roast
pig and Bank of Hell money
for the New Year,
early call for six o'clock mass,
notice of a new medium
strong on past lives.

And a yellow alert: in the news:
Woman Drowned in Sun Yee Pond,
a suicide. Avoid that area
the next hundred days.
Her ghost looks for a replacement,
her soul seeks release
from the water.

It is well the residents
of the Chinese Mind do not
debate dogmas. They practice
politenesses, are tolerant
of weird visitors
in their corridors.

III

MRS. WEI'S GARDEN

Mr. Wei Has No Respect

for the Gods, said Mrs. Wei.
At Ch'ng Ming he sits on tombstones,
walks around on graves.

I have to offer apologies and incense
on his behalf to pacify their occupants.
On New Year and all the festivals

when I pray and offer food
to the Gods, he shouts
from the dining hall "Hurry up!

The gods have tasted enough.
The food will get cold.
I'm hungry!"

Mrs. Wei on the Bus

found a seat thankfully set down her bags.
Hot bodies jostled her: schoolgirls in blue,
women shoppers, salesmen, a monk

carrying his alms pouch. A schoolgirl
near him struggled towards the exit.
She stumbled over Mrs. Wei's bags.

Mrs. Wei helped her up. "Why are you
leaving? You just got on. Are you
feeling sick?"

Eyes wide, the girl shook her head.
"No—he—the Monk touched me.
I'll catch the next bus."

Mrs. Wei rose in wrath, hissed to the girl
to watch her bags and began to bellow.
"Lecher! Animal! Reptile in saffron robe!

Secret Eater of Forbidden Meat!
Molesting young girls on buses!
I'll report you to your Abbot,

you vomit on Buddha's face!"
Eyes turned. Heads turned. In silence,
he took the path that opened to the exit.

"Always carry a safety-pin." Mrs. Wei said
to the schoolgirl, "When scum like that
surfaces, stab it in the ass.

That jackal is going to be
a lizard in his next life.
May Lord Buddha have mercy on his soul."

Mrs. Wei and the Goddess of Latrines

Too much attention embarrasses
the Goddess of Latrines. She's very shy.
That's why no one prays to her anymore.

I remember her at New Year. I burn
a stick of incense in the toilet.
She did me a favor once.

Men Yu, my first-born, was so sickly
his first hundred days of life.
I burnt slippers around his cradle,

put stones in the front door, but
the thou-tzu ghosts were not scared.
They were hungry and strong.

Each morning he was sicker, weaker.
My mother said, "Put him in the latrine.
Maybe the Goddess will hide him

from those childless ghosts."
Men Yu stayed in the bathroom
till he passed his hundred days.

Then the thou-tzu were powerless.
So I remember the Goddess at New Year.
More attention would scare her away.

Mrs. Wei Refuses to Bury Her Grandmother

The feng shui is no good on this plot.
The geomancer says the slope
is bad, the luck will wash away.

Old Master Ko died last year. The
feng shui of his grave was good.
See how fast his family business grows.

Burial in this spot will bring
sorrow to the family, poverty,
or the birth of daughters.

Grandmother will have to be cremated.
We can keep her ashes on a temple shelf
until a better plot becomes available.

Thirteen Is Terrible, Mrs. Wei Said

It took four miracles, one per
child, to raise my first four
past that unlucky age.

Each had to be hospitalized
during the thirteenth year:
Men Yu for jaundice, his skin turned

yellow as a monk's saffron robe.
Then Lan Li got under a pot
of boiling water. They peeled

the puffed skin off her legs
at the hospital. I swore I'd never
say "I'll skin you alive" again.

Then the mysterious sickness
that made Men Ya swell and swell.
The doctors shook their heads.

I went to Kuan Yin's temple.
The medium said Third Grandaunt's ghost
wanted his soul to keep her company.

So I took a stone from her grave
saying "I reclaim what belongs
to me." Men Ya recovered

after he drank the soup I made
with that stone. I burnt a paper doll,
a boy, to keep Grandaunt happy.

When Lan Fa had pneumonia
at thirteen, I realized the presence
of the Thirteenth Doorway Demons.

I promised Kuan Yin a roast
suckling pig, gold and silver
for her protection against them.

After that, none of the other
children had problems. If I had known
sooner, I'd have had fewer nights of fear.

Mrs. Wei Slaps Her Daughter's Hand

Don't throw that string away!
It can still be used.
Your dead grandfather, the scholar,
always said: By the river,
don't waste water. By the forest,
don't waste wood.
The Earth Gods watch their gifts.
They take them back from wastrels.

He also said: Wealth will not last
three generations in one family.
The first grabs it, the second
saves it, the third spends it.
Look at the Lu family.

Old Mr. Lu still rides
his creaky bicycle to his shop.
His grandsons go in chauffeured cars.
Their children will walk
to bus-stops and envy others.
The gleam of gold fades
from Ancestor Lu's bones,
it rises in another's.

Mrs. Wei and the Holy Water

In '62, a rumor rilled through
our town of a miraculous spring
by the railroad.

No one had witnessed its cures
but everyone knew about the spring
by sundown.

We washed and sterilized
bottles and congregated
there the next day

and the next, slowing down
all the trains. Some profiteers
sold bottles to passengers

as the trains inched by.
Soon everyone in town had a bottle
of holy water for home use. Then

the spring dried up. I suspect
the Railroad Company piped it somewhere else.
Weeks later, I found wrigglers

in my water and threw it out
without testing its powers.
I should have boiled it first.

Mrs. Wei and the Basket Spirit

You put chopsticks through the handles
of a used basket, hang the chopsticks
high on chairs and invite a spirit in.

Basket spirits are usually nice
gossips, women ghosts who help
pass an afternoon pleasantly.

Was Father happy in his new
house in Ghost Village? Did he live
with my mother or his first wife?

Which number will win the lottery?
Is there wealth in my near future?
Does my husband keep a mistress?

Many afternoons I invited
a spirit in to visit. Most were
glad to chat, sometimes a grumpy one

roused from her nap, would come,
rocking short and seldom, wanting
only to leave. No fun at all.

Then one came who refused to leave.
It jumped off its chopstick holder
when I tried to say goodbye.

It was friendly as a puppy
after meat scraps, wobbling after me
as I backed into the kitchen.

Holy Mountains! the idea of life
with a basket at my heels—such
embarrassment! Holy Mountains!

It took an hour of sweet talk
while I lied and sweated before
it left. No more spirit games for me.

Mrs. Wei and the Beggar

Sunday morning filled with quiet
and sleepers, this beggar rattles
his tin cup at our gate.

He is tall, once had muscles,
his eyes are stained
with opium yellow.

I put ten cents in his cup
feeling kind on this gentle day.
He picks it out and spits at it

and me. The nerve, when twenty
buys a meal of hot noodles,
a half-loaf of bread

with a paper of jam to go.
He curses me for mocking
a sick man

calls on gods in earth and sky
to ill-gift me and mine.
He makes such a din banging

his dented cup on my wrought-iron gate
I consider turning
the garden hose on him.

He makes such a din he wakes
Mr. Wei who erupts from the house
in red pajamas and a black face

and spews threats like a fumarole.
As he runs from Mr. Wei, that beggar
looks very healthy.

Mrs. Wei and Modern Marriage

Nowadays people are more romantic;
they kiss and cuddle even after
marriage. It looks very nice.

The men of my generation
kiss only low women. Couples
are water buffalo in a plow.

Now plows are easily dropped,
the buffalo run wild after kissing
while we stay in our fields.

Mr. Wei and I have never kissed.
Luckily he is more interested
in high cuisine than low women.

Mrs. Wei and the Thief

When I heard the rooster scream,
the hens in noisy panic, I knew
a thief was in my chicken house.

Grabbing a flashlight and a rattan cane
I ran to see a six-foot cobra,
patterned like woven grass, leave

with my best layer in its mouth.
It flowed swift as runnel water
into the cemetery behind the shed.

I followed, jumping over graves.
"Excuse me, please excuse" I said
to placate any ghosts about to rise.

I caught up to that jewelled spatula-head,
flailed it with my cane until
its gleaming eyes dulled,

then dragged its limpness to the road,
and stretched it across to be killed again,
its bright green pounded black

by passing cars, the sure way to kill
snake magic. Then I took my chicken
home to dinner.

Mrs. Wei Feeds Her Children

Eat your rice.

Lan Fa, watch your chopstick hand,
keep your palm up. Never
turn the back of your hand to Heaven,
the Gods will mark you for rebellious thoughts.

Men Yu, come back! You left ten
grains of rice in your bowl. You'll offend
the God of Planting. Do you want
to put pockmarks on the face
of your future wife?

IV

PRIVATE LANDSCAPE

Po Chu-I Looks Back

(The T'ang Dynasty poet is confined to his bed after his legs are paralysed, 842 A.D.)

It is kind of you to come
so far to see me. Sit there,
we can watch the sun set and drink
my new plum wine. Your voice
is better than any medicine.
                              Dear Friend,
there is no cause for sadness.
I shall manage, from time to time,
to go abroad. What matters most
is an active mind, not active feet.
By land I can ride a sedan chair,
by water, be rowed in a boat.

In dreams, I stride
over mountains, my legs tireless,
Yuan Chen by my side in eight-li boots.
I shed tears on waking, not for lost legs
but for my lost friend.
At Hsien-yang, ten autumns have swept
his grave-mound bare. No more poems
will his brush sweep across a page.
Even his fame is dead. His poems
deep in dust at the bottom
of boxes and cupboards.

We met in Ch'ang-an. He was
twenty-two, I almost thirty.
Five years we bonded our tie, roamed
on horseback, walked in the snow.

We recited verses to each other
over cups of warm wine, wandered
the Lands of Drunkenness together.
I can taste those days again
in early morning dreams.

No, I do not miss the days
of public office. I do not miss
the chill of dawn outside the Palace,
wet snow trickling into my thin
ceremonial shoes, rolling out praise
for the Emperor's passage.
I envied Ma Chen then. He turned down
all offices, slept warm
in eiderdown and bedsocks while I
and other ambitious fools
courted influenza by the Five Gates.

My ambitions died soon enough.
The Son of Heaven would not see me.
His favorites hated my satires
that exposed their corruption.
They used two harmless poems
to get me banished to Hsun-yang,
far from my friends,
far from Yuan Chen.

The gifts I sent to achieve recall.
It took six years. To my sadness,
Yuan Chen was banished before my return.

It was seven long years before
we met again, only to part after
one night.
                    One night we spent
unwrapping words from seven years.
When we turned our horses,

his to the North and the Shang
Mountains, mine south to Ch'ang-an,
our eyes were red.

The two poems? My mother drowned
in a well, bending to look
at flowers. I wrote "The New Well"
and "In Praise of Flowers"
years after her death. They served
to banish me. Have more wine.
It is from my own recipe.
Do you care for music? I have
two dancing girls. They sing
"The Willow Branch" rather well.
A frivolous poem, but I am pleased
it has become so popular.
Yes, I hear my "Everlasting Wrong"
has gained much fame. Do you know
Captain Kao's story?

He was courting a dancing girl
in the capital. She said "I
am no ordinary dancing girl.
I can recite Master Po's
'Everlasting Wrong.' " And
she put up her price.

Thank you. It is kind of you
to praise it. But it is not
a serious work.
                         It saddens me
that my satires, my heart-felt
poems seeking reforms, relief
for the common people, found
no response; they achieved
only my frequent departures
from the capital.

I am a filial subject to my Emperor.
But the Son of Heaven has turned
his ear from me.

Heaven knows I have been
a filial son, a good brother,
not always a fond father.
                    I offended Heaven
when Golden Bells was born. Aged
forty, I questioned the gods why
I had a child so late. I resented
the new responsibility.

I had been viewing with eagerness
an idle life, sleeping late, good talk
with friends and poets.
Now, I would have to put off
retirement another fifteen years
till she could put up her hair.
And then, have the trouble
of getting her married.
                    Heaven punished me.
She crossed the Yellow Springs
when she was two and I had grown
attached to her.

My only son, A-tsui was born
when I reached fifty-three.
Heaven took him back after
two short years. The ties of flesh
and bone only bind us to grief.
And pain.

I keep no more wives.
My wives were girls from good families.
They ran my house well, threw
no tantrums. Still, wives want time

and attention. Dancing girls
are easier, they demand trifles:
a little applause, a servant or two.

Yes, I still write. It is
my one weakness. Each time
I see a fine landscape, or encounter
a friend, a fresh flower, I recite
a new poem and am glad.
As if a god had looked me in the face.

Sometimes, I make a serious poem.
Yuan Chen would have praised it
but his bones lie clean and bare.
He was a Prince of friends. There was
no one like him in my life.

I used to climb to the Eastern Rock,
recite my work to the valley and hill.
I cannot do that anymore.

Still, my heart has spirit enough
to listen to harps and songs. At leisure
I open new wine, taste many cups.
                    Drunken, I recall old poems,
sing a whole volume.

Last year, I made a box
for my anthologies.
Seventy of them, three thousand poems.
I cannot bear to think they
will be lost and scattered. I know
the fate of poems, and poets.
I will divide them among my daughters.
Perhaps my grandchildren will treasure them.

An artist came last month.
The young fool wanted to paint
my portrait for posterity.
I said "Why waste your talent
on the crumpled face and withered limbs
of a sick man? My name is not
on the walls of Chilin Palace,
my works not mentioned in the Academy."
I sent him away with his brushes dry.
My best works were scorned.
I will not accept meaningless
recognition, now or posthumously.

No, no. I am not bitter. Well,
only a little. Only when fools
bring my failures to mind.

My days are spent pleasantly.
I rise late, have bamboo shoots
and rice for lunch. I could never
get enough bamboo shoots at Lo-yang.
Here, they are so cheap, I eat them
recklessly every day.

After lunch, I nap. When I wake,
I sit and watch the flowers. I read
until my eyes are sore.
My shroud suit is sewn. I know
my life's skein has run out of years.
When the Yellow Emperor summons,
I will rise and go without turning
my head backward. I hope
Yuan Chen can come to meet me
on the other bank of the Yellow Springs.

(Po Chu-I died four years later in 846 A.D.)

V

CAVES

Portrait of Miss Emily Dickinson

(with love and a little malice)

In the middle of afternoon tea, she was
holding a half-bitten cucumber sandwich
to catch a certain slant of light,
when the butler brought, on proper silver,
Mister W.J. Death's calling card.
She assumed he was a gentleman, though
their acquaintance was only to bow
in passing. This promised a new intimacy.

She laid aside her unfinished bread,
pressed white knuckles to a flutter
suddenly in her eyelids. She gathered up
her carriage robe and accepted,
with properly modest smile, Mister Death's
polite invitation to ride.

La la li dum pong

Che'gu Nariman force-fed
us Malay an hour each day.
"Bintang, binatang, kelapa, kepala:
Star, animal, coconut, head."
la la li dum pong.

"Che'gu Nariman weighs three hundred pounds,
Che'gu Nariman sweats in the dark,
Che'gu Nariman sleeps in the park,
mashes benches into the ground..."
Good morning, Che'gu Nariman.

Che'gu Nariman breaks her chalk,
whacks her cane,
spoons out adverbs, proverbs.
senyap: quiet, chakap: talk.
"Kechil Nakal, Besar Gatal!"

She'd whip out her favorite threat:
"Little imps into sex-starved sirens grow."
Che'gu died, and left her all
to nineteen cats.
la la li dum pong.

Spacey Spiders

Spiders like spacing:
two arachnid astronauts
were observed to spin
webs delicate
and complex
concocting whorls, spirals,
radials, trajectories so intricate
Arachne would gladly hang
herself over again
to concede their superiority.

Reports have it they died
of dehydration and aridity
on returning earthside.
I know better, I listen to roses:
they refused gravity and suicided
on fine silken hoses.

Science Fiction Fantasia

for Cheryl Dorall

I've had it with John Wyndham, Larry Niven,
Lewis, Bradbury and Asimov too.
I'm through with Merrill, Herbert, Heinlein
and the whole science fiction crew.

I used to thrill to sacrificing parents
who killed their offspring in sorrow and fear
because they heard on Doomsday Radio
the Big Bang was inevitable, was near.

I used to swallow all that pap with ease:
nuclear devastated futures, men in caves
mutated past recognition, deformed by disease,
grimly scavenging fodder out of graves.

I'm sick of hearing that automation,
pollution, dehumanization lies ahead, and how!
I'm tired of horrors, desperation, degradation;
there's enough in newspapers now.

I'd rather escape with Marion Bradley nee Zimmer
to where hocus-pocus is science under the Bloody Sun,
where telekinesis, telepathy and magics are simple
but wait, what if I landed there with no 'laran'?

I would fly a fire-breathing bronze dragon
or command a flight of fire-lizards on thread-scored Pern.
Only problem: I may end up a coarse peasant
that any reptile worth its oil would spurn.

I'd like to be a jet-setter witch of Karres
having fun with a vatch on a time-tunnel jig.
I'm just afraid I'd transmigrate into a Fed. nasty
and be turned into a schizophrenic pig.

I'd settle for being lovelorn Lois Lane
for a few super flings with Superman
but I fear to end up her nurse in old age
spooning her gruel and sterilizing her bed pan.

I think I'd best give up reading,
keep all six feet upon the ground.
I'll sit and watch magugurgles feeding
off willawallies in their short merry round.

Fairy Tales

My mother told me fairy tales
of fair gentle maids who loved and gained
strong handsome princes, heroic males.

These muscle-bound heroes grew stale,
their perfection each story's refrain.
My mother told me fairy tales

where heroes made monsters turn tail,
yet never bothered to rescue plain
farmers' daughters. These honorable males

left good-natured sidekicks to rot in jails
while they rode a magic carpet or crane
to wed rich princesses. Fairy tales

of marriages without quarrels, travails.
They loved faithfully, never complained
of lumpy thighs, the high price of retail.

They never had hemorrhoids or hangnails,
didn't suffer pimples or grumble at the rain.
My mother told me fairy tales:
strong handsome princes, heroic males.

Cinderella on an ordinary day

"I like my body when it is with your body..."

e.e.cummings

Waiting
for water
to boil

is waiting

for you to unmask
your feelings.

Midnight.
When I turn
into a pumpkin,
you are there
with a glass
slipper.

Yet in sometime places when
our clocks agree
ohyesIlikemybodywithyourbodywhen

you
are there
behind your eyes.

You My Husband

Raise your eyes beyond the shiftings and
scrimpings, your account in the Savings & Loan,
for the living daylight fades in your hand.

The white mare paws at your gate, you stand
juggling business deals upon black phones.
Raise your eyes. Beyond,   the shifting sand

buries starfish and mating eels. Look, man
making land and securities your cornerstones
for living, daylight fades in your hand.

You call three shirts ostentation, can't stand
feminists, liberals, interest-free loans.
Raise your eyes beyond the shifting sand.

Sea-lions call, dripping mermaids demand
entry at your door, the swelling wave foams
as the living daylight fades.   In your hand

the money-counting years grimly span
hard cash, bonds, they unflesh your bones.
Raise your eyes beyond the shifting sand
for the living day. Light fades in your hand.

Our Room's Splendour Is Not In

its furniture: two chests, candles
in molded brass to make
small radiances, an ample bed.
Two bedside clocks to count
minutes we drop from our hands,
freeing them for each other.
Time we unnumbered together
talking or not talking in bed.

You write you fondle stone
statues in Moghul palaces,
that you miss my alabaster thighs,
that winter is spring in India.
It is strange to think of you
in unreal two-dimensioned places
out of scenic picture books,
to know you walk, talk, sleep not here.

Our room is alien without you.
Dust creeps up the candle wicks. The clocks
have become misers and nags. Outside
the snow falls. The room is cold.

Glad Consequence

for Ilana

Glad consequence of our two bodies'
delight in each other,
the nights we lit moon lanterns,
unknowing we kindled you.
Now we hold up names like candles
to match your cometlight.
Grinning like idiots we turn
to each other, amazed
that six pounds of our blood and bone
should make this ordinary
world shine and shine.

Night Flowers

I am running, running knowing
I am too late. My daughter drowns
smiling as she plummets into
icy water.

I am running, running knowing
I cannot prevent: my daughter
laughs as she trips and breaks
on a field of glinting shards,
broken bottles, mirrors.

I hold a limp body emptied of my child.

Screams well up my throat. Silence
presses them down until my throat splits
and I wake, gagging. My ears hear
only a sleeping house.

She breathes. She is alive.

It takes days as she runs,
shouts, fights with her sisters
before the corpse surrounded by
malevolent glass fades into the ground.

I set to with spade to dig
out guilt that grows such flowers, glad to lean
on Freud: night flowers root in the past.
I shudder away ancestral voices. They whisper:
these are shadows thrown from the future.

The Hard Bed

She presses toward the ceiling
pulling taut the transparent cord
that leashes her to the body on the bed.
She watches with detachment
the spilling of her body's
fluids into the catheter bag.
Her body is spread out before her eyes
clear as diagrams in an anatomy text;
its intricate system of pipes,
convoluted tubes, bleed valves,
drain valves, multiple closings
and openings so narrow, blockage seems
inevitable, a master plumber's nightmare.

She has been in hospitals before,
each time a loss. Once the ten week child,
large as her fist, eyes and hands already formed.
She had drowned in her womb's darkness
night after night swimming after her child.
Now the uterus is gone, its space
filled by a well of pain.

She becomes aware of others, like her,
faint shapes perched above their bodies,
waiting until feeling
becomes bearable.

The Woman Searching For Her Unborn Child

She is walking
under endless canopies of swords
woven with bayonets, sharpened
stakes that rustle, ready
to fall on her upturned face.
Weapons of some lost battle singing
their unfinished song filling
the dim corridor smoky
smell of hunger, an urgency for moist flesh.
Damocles only had one sword, she thinks
over and over to the drumbeat in her head.

She cannot bear
the terrible thirst that sucks
at her eyes
but she cannot look aside.
Those bundles cannot be, are
not fetuses, they look like
half-formed babies. Those are not
skulls behind skin walls
rattling their loose teeth gaping
cavities at her. You cannot
see through walls. Pinch yourself!
Pinch yourself awake! her mind cries.
She wakes and the bayonets close in.

Choices

For sins of negation and aborted chance
we toss and burn, sleepless in the dark
for lives we uprooted before they could take.
We could have been kind to the living
child with grandmother's face, now dead,
plucked from seeds of other faces ready to fall.

Sooner or late, the speckling leaves fall
from the tree to lie until chance
winds stir them. They simulate the dead.
Blind worms find their pyres in the dark,
spin their veins and cells into living
threads the oak and sycamore will take.

The foxglove and maidenhair fern too will take
them to infuse leaves with green until Fall,
tumbling them on a spoke of the living
wheel forever unless dislodged by chance
or deliberately raked into hot dark
incinerators to become truly dead.

Trees bend over their dead,
ghost roots follow them as they take
the spiralling path into the dark,
past dinosaur bones, Devonian ferns. They fall
until earth heaves, random chance,
and rolls them up toward the living,

spins them past the living
rooted in the planet's skin. The dead
cannot know or care they chance

to rise. Insensate, they take
the ghost ride skyward, thin dark
motes borne forever in free fall.

We remember our lost futures in Fall
as beauty breaks from the living
and color vanishes into the dark
uncolor of Night. We smell the dead
on her black shield. Memories take
us by the throat. We wait for another chance.

Now we are ready. The chance will fall
to others to take into their arms living
children. Our dead open us in the dark.

Grass

Tell me, have you watched the grass grow?
In moonlight, encouraged by a motherly wind.
Some night when you need to escape
mobbing thoughts, walk into a green patch
silvered in star-shadows and rest your weary head;
quiet your clamoring siren of a mind
and see each blade arch its slender wand.
Listen to the slither of grass stretching,
fingering out strands of shadow
on the dark warm earth, as waves and
waves of moonlight wash over them
and over you—soaking your splintered brain
and sedating—for a time at least—all pain
and all sorrow.
And when you wake from the anaesthesia
which is only a moment in time but
seems all time, you will realise
the day-trodden grass is grotesque at night.

Working Women

Metro stops mark our days.
March, December winds blow us
clutching at lamp-posts
into the underground, hustle us
into overheated offices.
January snows feather-whip us.
Blinking, we trudge to work, stamp
mud-brown prints on winter white
that melt and slush into sludge
of discarded days.

Summer's a haze of hurried packings,
lost beach balls, misplaced suntans.
We cannot remember what we did
with the small change counted
into our hands by clocks.
Only Fall is clear: sweeping mountains
bare and blue, strumming colors off the trees,
splashing the air with ripe apple cologne,
unwrapping each day to sparkle in windows.

We are surprised by the quick departure
of the year, confused by the news'
rude arrival. We had no time
to prepare a proper perspective.
The separate days run unnoticed
into unmemorable waste and a huge bill.
Now and then we pause, we speak
of inner weather.

Jake

Helmet, gloves, Harley Davidson:
the Jake I remember
in the Peace Corps.
You spun miles upon the wind,
the beat of your bike's thunder
shaking up villages and chicken coops,
scaring snakes and monkeys
back into the jungle.

You were always
so serious, wanting
to commit
yourself
to each girl so new.
"Marry me" you cried
as you launched out
into that wonderful green
unknown, love.

In Hajai you learned Thai
to propose to Girl No. 47
in the Red Star Massage Parlor.
"Love transcends languages" you said
rapt in a girl with no name.
John talked you out of it then.

I burst the balloon when
you told me you planned
to marry Pam, loosing
words I would recall.
"You mean Pam the Pincushion?"

You married Marita and found
it was not love you hungered for.
It was falling, danger that you craved.
I hear you've taken up hang gliding
and Tibetan languages.

Carol's Poem

I was your childwife.
I grew up fast
when you locked me out
    of our house
    our past.
You were kind enough your way
sent my battered case of memories
you had no room for them, you said.
There are new occupants,
    do keep in touch
    (but out of sight, please.)

My new apartment is austere
I've stopped filling it with remnants
am peaceful now with emptiness.
    A certain beauty lurks
    in bare walls, nakedness,
        sitting on the floor.
I fill a bigger space than I knew,
I've been so used to squeezing into closets
    with you turning the key.

Sunlight no longer hurts my albino eyes.
Your shadows recede, slowly, it is true.
But I can see rooftops, trees, blue sky
    over the blades of grass.
I think I may walk past the cemetery gate
    and out into the town today.

Michal

(Daughter of King Saul, King David's first wife)

One hundred foreskins from the Philistines
for her bride price, my father said, hoping
for your death.

You flung at his feet twice the number.
How I rejoiced to be your bride.
I would have stripped the sky
of stars, plucked the moon at your desire.

When my father sent assassins in the dark,
I saved your life, forgetting loyalty
to father, brothers.

To avenge your escape, my father decreed me
unwed, gave me to Paltiel. I was hawk
with your hawk, I became dove with Paltiel.
He netted me with softness, made me
kind and gentle for a while. Paltiel,
who walked after me, wept after me
when I departed, spoil of war, possession
you reclaimed as new King.

I saw you, coming into Jerusalem, leaping
like an epileptic goat, skirts lifted high
dangling your manhood for all to see,
randy travesty of kingship.

I met you with harsh words and won
your anger. And the words we no longer speak

have lain together and begotten hard black moths
to eat holes in my heart.

When God sent the famine, you let the rabble
of Gibeon hang my seven brothers, sacrifice
Saul's last seed, left their bodies
swinging in the barley harvest. Their mother,
mad Rizpah, with sticks and stones, kept
the carrion vultures from their bodies.
You relented for her sake. But you buried them
too late. The vultures have come to my roof
and we wait for God to forsake you, David.
As he abandoned Saul.

The Boy

The only time his mother said
"yes" to his father was at night
locked within their bedroom.
He must be beating her
for calling him "Fool" all day,
the boy thought.
He liked his father then, hearing
her yesses shrill through
the wall between their rooms.

He dreaded mornings, knowing
his father would mumble yesses
in daylight while she prowled
for faults and errors.

Older, learning he was wrong,
his father did not beat her at night,
the boy shaped himself never to have
a woman say yes to him in the dark
for in the clarity of morning
she would call him "Fool."

Night of the Barbarian

In the space
between the taking out of trash cans
and the locking of the door,
the stranger slipped into her house,
slammed shut his trap.

                                    Outside,
crickets are singing, groping
in dark grass for grain.
Outside, black-capped
catbird pecks, rips cricket
guts, crushes fluttering legs,
cracks, splits, splatters
thin shells, gulps down
cricket gel in a catbird dream.
And a field mouse, plucked
from feeding in the trash, flails
weak cries into the talons of a shrike.

Safe in a cave in the ceiling, she
watches the dream of rape unreel, watches
a gorilla hooded in black stocking
gibber on her belly, claw her
knees into the rug, watches her body
spiral apart, her voice spray the air
with sawdust, her hands rise, break,
rise and again disintegrate.

Shrinking into cave spider, she spins
sheath upon web sheath to endure
the passage of this dream.

When she wakes, she will
find legs, hair, skin,
ears, lungs; tie them back with string.

She will tie
knots upon knots. She will search,
she will not find
the world the barbarian crushed
under his hand tonight.

Three Revolts of Miss Maybury

I'm tired of
my primeval state
Eve lacking Adam's rib
too bright fruit that cling
around unfleshed hips
serpents writhe
I declare
winter
Snow it

waiting
decaying
spring betrayed
to fall
weary
in wasted hands
I will haul
for hope city
with indifference

Miss Maybury Takes a Nap

Her legs arranged
neatly, toes keeping the
ceiling at bay, she
folds down her eyes
sinks
through the mattress the floor the concrete
into the ground
spreading her limbs far, wide
expanding each pore
to match the interstices
between grit and grain
flowing into ground water into
mist into air
feeling clouds trickle between
drops of cold on her palms
green fragrance of grass.
                              Rivers turn
into her mouth, slice into
clumps of hills, gush forth
from eye sockets. Her smiling teeth
are boulders now, breaking
water into whiteness that aches.
Grass roots spear through
her blackening skin, they brandish
flowers, white flags. Suddenly
there are butterflies
in battalions, steel wings
cutting her cobweb body
into sparkling wisps.

World War II Soldier's Cemetery, Kuala Lumpur, 1983

Forty years ago, this patch of
unwanted ground was used
to hold the corpses of Japanese
invaders, alien in the moisture-
burdened heat, alien in their mottled-
green suits, alien in the leached
laterite of the conquered land.

The soil is no longer red. Their
humanity has turned it richly
black. Still this land is unwanted:
an untouched memory of the war
gentled in the tall green
obscurity of grass.

crows in the cemetery

who watch with yellowing eyes
the coming of many corteges
their voices crying "all, all."

Seeds

In the sparse shade of a dying
sycamore, a woman on a hard bench
sits, looking at sparrows
scrounge seeds from the scanty grass.

She'd heard that grass seeds pass
through their gullets to grow
green in other places, yet had never
seen soft turf outside cultivated lawns.

She'd heard of sons surviving the war.
Her only son returned wrapped in a flag.
She cannot extract warmth from flags or
from the late summer sun anymore,
nor from thoughts that fine green seeds
may be growing in Vietnam.

Refugees—China Sea

Typhooning sea
immovable sky
pressed
our small boat
into bristling waves.
Waters coiled and
uncoiled, laughed at our
helplessness.

The rough
hands of
pirates claimed us,
picked us over,
raped us,
then shoved us
prowing north
stubborn to survive,
to chew splintered wood,
salvage saliva,
to be swept back
to the conquered land we paid
heavy gold to
quit.

Two Inches

For thirty-two days we held that thought
a shield before our eyes:
Two inches of paper sea to cross, to reach
freedom.

In the fog of sweat, vomit, hunger cramps,
we saw page ten on the school atlas:
Two inches of sea to cross, to get
to Indonesia.

Back when we scrabbled for rice the soldiers
spilled in the dirt,
Two inches of sea to cross to free us
from oppression.

Back when they raped our mouths for gold,
our hidden map comforted us:
Two inches of South China Sea to cross,
to freedom.

We did not know two inches of water
could hold so many storms, so many pirate
ships, so many ways of dying.

Statistics

(the Dung Thi Nguyen family)

all our lives we have known war

Haiphong
        we were fishers, the sea fed us well

1954   the Communists came

Phan Thiet
        we built another boat

1968   the Communists came

Vung Tau
        there were whales they brought luck
        we had good years

1975   the Communists won the war

Seadrift, Texas
        they did not like us fishing
        their waters

Biloxi, Mississippi

        we hope
        we can stay

To the Sponsor of a Vietnamese Family

Do not scold
when we buy chicken so often,
we have not seen meat for three years.

You are angry with us,
sad we are not sensible
our children eat too much candy.

You plan a budget,
a diet we do not follow.
In such small ways we taste freedom again.

Remembering Ho Chi Minh City

The war was over. The victors came.
Vietcong looking just like us wearing guns,
slinging insults. We could take that.

They stripped us, looking for jewels,
poured laxatives down our throats.
They smashed in our walls for possible caches.

They kicked us when we were on our knees
scrabbling for rice they spilled in the dirt
as they took away our harvest.

They ripped silver fillings from our mouths,
laughed when they found gold; their faces
horror-house mirrors of our faces.

Cambodian Refugees
National Geographic, *May, 1980*

my eyes keep slipping
clutch at the printed words

avoid the photograph of a skeleton
breathing in its sheath of skin

angles of bone that jut through skin
flatness of skin that cleaves to bone

how the heart writhes
    a grass snake caught in a fire.

Millet Seed

In the beginning, the people
buried their dead on distant hills
giving their ghosts pots of food, rain
        for water, quiet existence
away
        from the noisy living.

The little children they kept
in shallow beds around the house, near
    the thrum of daylight feet,
        the clatter of pans
            and mother voices.
After burial, small hands reach out of the grass,
grope to touch warm familial feet.

The mother pounds dry millet
in her stone mortar, keeps her tears
out of the sun-yellow flour.
        Suddenly, she is running,
running out into the fields, urgent to press
the sweat-slick arms of the father. He turns
loam, works cutoff stalks
back into the soil for spring planting.